The King Who Rained

by FRED GWYNNE

Aladdin Paperbacks

Aladdin Paperbacks
An imprint of Simon & Schuster
Children's Publishing Division
1230 Avenue of the Americas New York, NY 10020
Copyright © 1970 by Fred Gwynne
All rights reserved including the right of reproduction in whole or in part in any form.
Originally published by Windmill Books, Inc. and Simon & Schuster, Inc.
Manufactured in the United States of America
17   16   15   14   13   12   11
Library of Congress Cataloging in Publication Data
Gwynne, Fred.
  The king who rained.
  SUMMARY: A little girl pictures the things her parents talk about, such as a king who rained, bear feet, and the foot prince in the snow.
  1. English language—Homonyms—Juvenile literature.   [1. English language—Homonyms]   I. Title.
PE1595.G75   1980   428.1   80-12939
ISBN 0-671-66744-0

1668 8044

Daddy says there was a king who rained for forty years.

there are forks in the road.

Daddy says
he has a mole
on his nose.

lambs gamble on the lawn.

Sometimes
Mommy says
she has a frog
in her throat.

Other times she says she's a little horse and needs the throat spray.

And when I give it to her,
she says I'm a little deer.

My big sister's getting married
and she says I can hold up her train.

Daddy says next time he paints the house he's going to give it two coats.

Daddy says there's
a head on his beer.

Daddy says all we get in the mail are big bills.

her when she's playing bridge.

Daddy says our family
has a coat of arms.

Daddy says we should
live in the present.

Mommy says little children
always have bear feet.

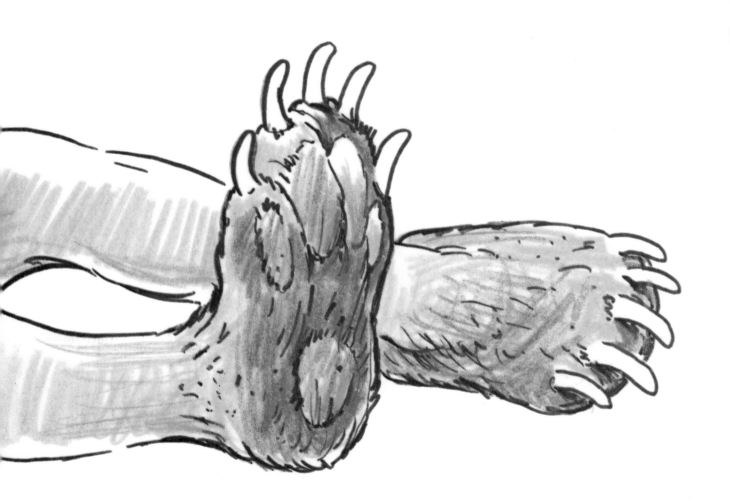

I've heard Daddy talk about the foot prince in the snow…

...and the blue prince for
the new room on our house.

Daddy says some boars
are coming to dinner.

Did you ever hear such a bunch of fairy tails?